For A.M.H. — Thanks for letting me share your story
Text Copyright © M.R. Nelson 2012 • Illustration Copyright © Tamia Sheldon 2012
First Bilingual Edition
All Rights Reserved. No portion of this book may be reproduced without express permission from the publisher.
ISBN: 9781623957674 • eISBN: 9781623957681
Published in the United States by Xist Publishing www.xistpublishing.com

Hora de Dormir en el Zoológico
The Zebra Said Shhh

M.R. Nelson Tamia Sheldon

It was bedtime at the zoo, but it was NOT quiet.
The animals were not sleeping.
They were all talking.
Up in his paddock, the zebra was very, very tired, but he could not go to sleep because of the noise.

So the zebra said, "Shhh, it's time to go to sleep."

Era la hora de dormir en el zoológico, pero NO había silencio. Los animales no estaban durmiendo. Todos estaban hablando.
Arriba en su potrero, la cebra estaba muy, muy cansada, pero no podía ir a dormir debido al ruido que había.

La cebra dijo "Shhh, es hora de dormir."

But the monkeys did not want to go to sleep.
They said, "ooo, ooo, ooo" and swung around the trees.
The zebra said, "Shhh, it's time to go to sleep."

Pero los monos no querían dormir.
Ellos decían "ooo, ooo, ooo", y se balanceaban por los árboles.
La cebra dijo "Shhhh, es hora de dormir."

The lion did not want to go to sleep.
He said, "raaar," and prowled around his den.

The zebra said, "Shhh, it's time to go to sleep."

El león no quería dormir.
Él decía "raar", y merodeaba por su guarida.

La cebra dijo "Shhh, es hora de dormir".

The parrot did not want to go to sleep.
She said, "squawk, squawk," and flew around amongst the leaves.

The zebra said, "Shhh, it's time to go to sleep."

La loro no quería dormir. Ella decía "squawk, squawk", y volaba entre las hojas.

La cebra dijo "Shhhh, es hora de dormir".

The turtles did not want to go to sleep.
They said, "snap, snap," and lumbered around the yard by their pond.

The zebra said, "Shhh, it's time to go to sleep."

Las tortugas no querían dormir.
Ellas decían "snap, snap", y se movían pesadamente en la yarda junto a su estanque.

La cebra dijo "Shhhh, es hora de dormir".

The seals did not want to go to sleep.
They said, "ar, ar," and splashed around
in their pool.

The zebra said,
"Shhh, it's time to go to sleep."

Las focas no querían dormir. Ellas decían "ar, ar",
y salpicaban en su piscina.

La cebra dijo "Shhh, es hora de dormir".

The giraffe did not want to go to sleep. She said, "munch, munch," and chewed on the leaves from her tree.

The zebra said, "Shhh, it's time to go to sleep."

La jirafa no quería dormir. Ella decía "munch, munch", y masticaba las hojas de su árbol.

La cebra dijo "Shhhh, es hora de ir a dormir".

The hippopotamus did not want to go to sleep. He said, "snort, snort," and rolled around in the mud by his pond.

The zebra said, "Shhh, it's time to go to sleep."

El hipopótamo no quería ir a dormir. Él decía "snort, snort", y se revolcaba en el lodo junto a su charco.

La cebra dijo "Shhhh, es hora de dormir".

The rhinoceros did not want to go to sleep. She went, "stamp, stamp," and stirred up the dust in her field.

The zebra said, "Shhh, it's time to go to sleep."

La rinoceronte no quería dormir. Ella decía "stamp, stamp", y agitaba el polvo en su campo.

La cebra dijo "Shhhh, es hora de ir a dormir".

The polar bear did not want to go to sleep.
He said, "grrrrr," and stalked around the ice.

The zebra said, "Shhh, it's time to go to sleep."

El oso polar no quería dormir.
Él decía "grrrrr", y acechaba en el hielo.

La cebra dijo "Shhhh, es hora de dormir".

Suddenly, it got very quiet at the zoo.
None of the animals were talking anymore.
They were all asleep!

De repente, el zoológico estaba en silencio.
Ninguno de los animales hablaba.
¡Estaban todos dormidos!

The monkeys were asleep
in their trees.

Los monos dormían en sus árboles.

The lion was asleep in his den.

El león dormía en su guarida.

The parrot was asleep in her nest amongst the trees.

El loro dormía en su nido en los árboles.

The turtles were asleep
by their pond.

Las tortugas dormían en su estanque.

The seals were asleep
by their pool.

Las focas dormían en su piscina.

The giraffe was asleep
by her tree.

La jirafa dormía junto a su árbol.

The hippopotamus was asleep
in the mud.

El hipopótamo dormía en el lodo.

The rhinoceros was asleep
in her field.

La rinoceronte dormía en su campo.

The polar bear was asleep
on the ice.

El oso polar dormía en el hielo.

And up in his paddock,
the zebra said, "Shhh,"
and he closed his eyes
and went to sleep.

Y arriba en su potrero, la cebra dijo
"Shhh", cerró sus ojos y se fue a dormir.

Made in the USA
Charleston, SC
10 April 2015